Wisdom Finds a Way

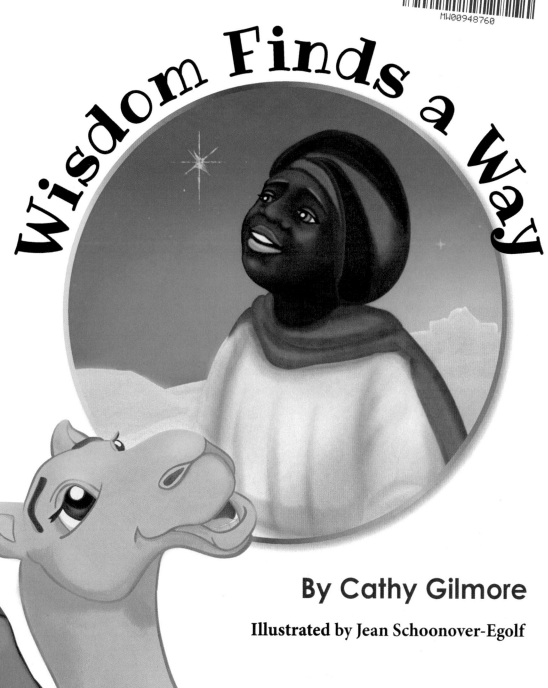

By Cathy Gilmore

Illustrated by Jean Schoonover-Egolf

Tiny Virtue Heroes™ Book 3: Team JOY

Wisdom Finds a Way:
The Virtue Story of Wisdom

First Edition: November 2020
ISBN 978-1-7356643-1-6

PERPETUAL LIGHT PUBLISHING

www.perpetuallightpublishing.com

Visit www.VirtueHeroes.com
to know more.

Bethlehem? My first time to be part of a big caravan and we are going to a tiny, little town. Hmmm.

For King Balthazar to travel hundreds of miles to such a tiny place, there must be a special reason. My master is very wise. This must be an important journey.

I'm Amel, a camel serving in King Balthazar's royal household. He is my hero. He sees what others miss, and he does what others don't do.

Balthazar says that the stars have been moving in new ways.

He and his father and grandfather before him studied God's story told in the stars.

Most of us just see stars as twinkling lights in the night.

But for **WISE** men, those lights mean so much more.

A great star has appeared.

He says the light is a sign that a promised King, a Messiah, has been born of a virgin. The stars are announcing the birth of a baby!

Balthazar and his friends, the kings Caspar and Melchior, planned to travel together on a great journey to honor the child. Each king comes with his own caravan with many supplies and servants.

Together, we are quite a group.

The light of the STAR will lead us.

Finally, the day arrives and we are on our way!

Since I'm a young camel and can't carry big parcels yet, I have the honor of carrying the gifts for the baby:

gold,

frankincense,

and

myrrh.

I don't understand how those things are the gifts for a baby.

The kings are a little mysterious, but I trust their judgement.

As we travel, King Caspar has a loving word or a caring touch for every person and animal he meets. His ancient eyes sparkle with kindness. "Your first journey, heh? You will do well. I remember when my Habibi was just a calf like you."

I'm no calf! I'm almost 7 years old. But I keep that thought to myself. I know I have a lot to learn.

Old Habibi the camel is sure-footed and kind. He gives me a wink and a grin. He seems to have a loving heart like his king.

After traveling many days and nights through the desert, we see a huge city shining ahead of us. Surely this will be the place to find a king!

I hope we find the comforts of home inside these walls.

To me, this looks like a great place for a **camel** to get a snack, a bath, and a bed of fresh straw.

As we enter the city, my king looks worried. Although the palace is beautiful, we can't see the light of our star.

Balthazar wants a rest, too. But he seems to sense darkness beneath the glitter of this gleaming place. I know him.

He will sacrifice his comfort to make sure we can safely complete our journey to find the baby King.

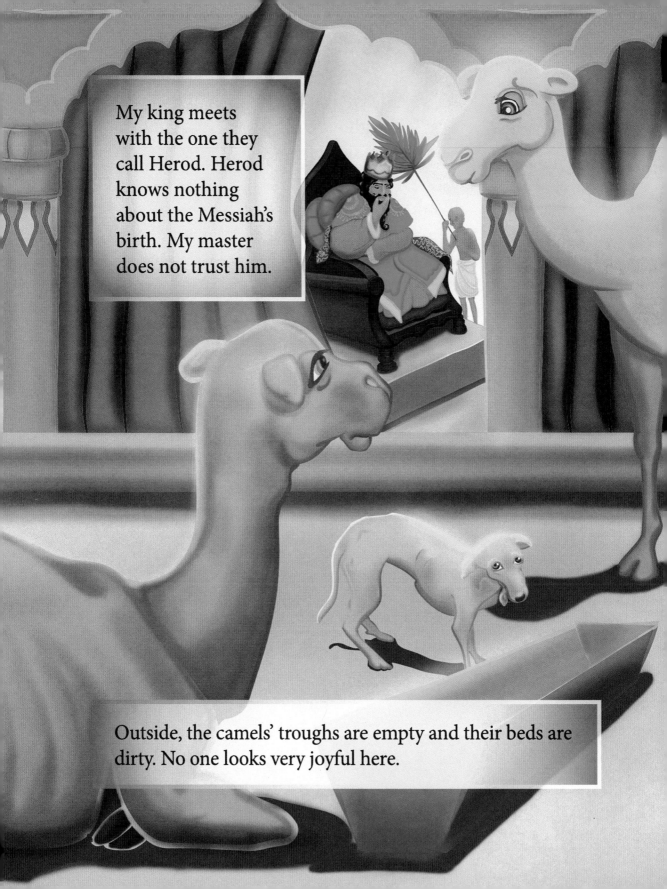

My king meets with the one they call Herod. Herod knows nothing about the Messiah's birth. My master does not trust him.

Outside, the camels' troughs are empty and their beds are dirty. No one looks very joyful here.

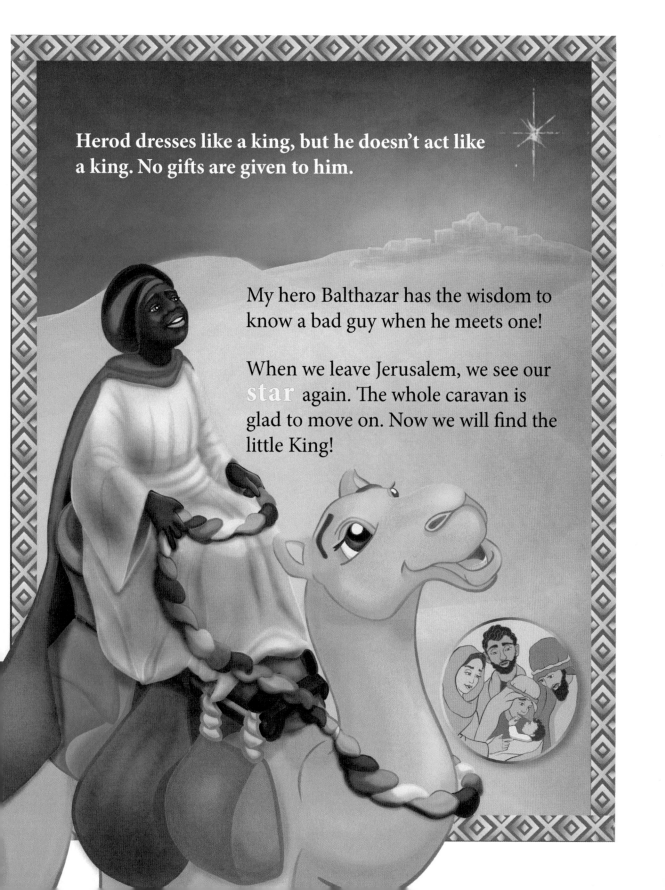

Herod dresses like a king, but he doesn't act like a king. No gifts are given to him.

My hero Balthazar has the wisdom to know a bad guy when he meets one!

When we leave Jerusalem, we see our star again. The whole caravan is glad to move on. Now we will find the little King!

The next day of our journey, King Melchior sings beautiful chants in a language I can't understand.

"What is he doing?" I ask Melchior's camel Gita.

"He is praying," she says.

"What is he praying for?"

"For God's help finding our way," Gita replies.

"But I thought all we have to do is follow the star," I say.

"Prayer for God's **grace**," says Gita, "gives us clarity to see what's hidden and to seek what's worthy of honor."

We all join in Melchior's melody. Chanting camels! Now that's something you don't hear every day.

The little town of Bethlehem is only a short distance away. We are almost there! As we get closer, I keep wondering, *How can anyone really tell if a baby is a king?*

It doesn't make sense to me, but Balthazar, Melchior, and Caspar are wise and good. They take good care of all of us. I trust that they know what they're doing.

That is, until I see Bethlehem.

Can this really be the place?

There is nothing royal about it! Why would anyone look for a long-awaited king--whose birth is announced by a giant star--in a tiny village like this? How will we know which home is his?

Suddenly, Caspar halts the caravan.

Excitedly, he says, "These shepherds know exactly where the baby King is staying! They have a field nearby where we can set up our tents."

God is answering our prayers!

Unlike Herod, these shepherds know all about the royal birth. They beam with happiness, and their joy is contagious.

We set up camp with the **shepherds**. A soft green pasture beats desert sand any day! Strangely, no one is putting on pajamas or bedding down for the night. What in the world is going on?

Instead of going to bed, Balthazar and the others begin dressing in their finest robes. Even Habibi, Gita, and the other camels are almost giddy with excitement.

Balthazar dresses me up! I must be the fanciest camel ever! I'm getting pretty excited to meet this Baby, too!

Maybe a king can hide inside of a child?

At dawn, the shepherds lead us to a **stable** built into a cave nearby. It is neat and tidy, and the animals seem happy.

Then I notice three people living in there! Can this be a king's family?

Joseph, the child's papa, welcomes us warmly. He doesn't look like a king on the outside, but he has a kind and respectful manner like my noble king.

They beckon all of us to come in and meet the Child!

Even us camels!

Now it is time to present our gifts.

Caspar, the oldest king in our caravan, is the
first to kneel before the tiny, holy Child.

He places his gift of
gold at the feet of the
Holy Family.

His wisdom
wrinkles scrunch up
around his eyes. The
LOVE on his
face shines brighter
than his gift.

*Perhaps a king can be hidden
inside a child whom someone
so wise can love so much.*

Melchior is next to humbly
bow and offer his gift.

He shyly approaches, barely
lifting his head. But his
voice! It fills the space with
music. His beautiful chant is
a song of gratitude to God.

Some grains of his
gift of frankincense
burn in a little pot. His
PRAYER lifts all
our thoughts to Heaven
with the sweet smoke.

*Perhaps a king can be
hidden inside a child
whom someone would
honor with such a
holy prayer.*

Finally, my master Balthazar comes before the Baby. He bows and offers his gifts, a vial of oil and a small tree with white blossoms.

Precious myrhh, an odd, but royal, gift for a baby. Myrrh is the oil used to anoint a king for burial when he dies.

My hero says he is ready to **SACRIFICE** his life for this Baby.

Perhaps a king can be hidden inside a child for whom noble Balthazar is willing to die.

The Holy Family humbly and gratefully accepts all the love and honor that the kings give with their gifts.

The joy of this moment with Jesus is an everlasting TREASURE for us all.

The kings and common folk alike delight in the little Child.

Bethlehem isn't fancy, but all who seek this **KING** are rich in love, generosity, and friendship.

When it's time to leave this humble and holy place, gift giving continues!

The kings give away nearly everything we brought with us.

That's a gift for which I'm grateful. I'll have less to carry on the trip home!

We say goodbye to Bethlehem with songs and smiles. As I look into the eyes of the little children around us, I think, *A wise and noble hero is hidden inside each child.*

That means YOU, my reader, are a royal son or daughter of the King of Heaven and Earth.

Thank you, God our Father, for giving your children the joyful gift of WISDOM to make us virtue-strong!

Hi Readers!

I'm a *not-so-tiny* Virtue Hero, a storyteller, a sidekick, and your friend. You can think of me as your play-time or pray-time partner. I tell everyone the virtue story of my hero Balthazar.

Balthazar is my hero because he shows me that Wisdom is the exercise of strong spiritual judgement that grows through love, prayer, and sacrifice. Balthazar isn't just *any* hero. He is a **virtue** hero of WISDOM.

VIRTUES

are the power of God's goodness alive in us. Prayer makes us VIRTUE STRONG.

Pray a prayer with me:

Dear God, our Father, Your Son became a tiny little one to save us all. Help me to be a Virtue Hero like wise Balthazar, even though I am small.

You can be a VIRTUE HERO!

When we ask God to guide what we **think** and **pray**, **do** and **say**, we enable holy habits like WISDOM to grow virtue-strong in us.

Balthazar shows us that God places the power to be loving, holy, and noble inside each of us. Seeking Jesus and his wisdom gives us virtue strength, and enables us to be Virtue Heroes™!

AMEL
CHARACTER CARD

Virtue Power: WISDOM, the use of knowledge to seek and do what is right

Virtue Color: SILVER

Tiny Virtue Hero Team: TEAM JOY

Favorite Story: The Nativity, when Jesus came into the world as a tiny baby king

Favorite BIBLE VIRTUE HERO: BALTHAZAR (one of the 3 kings who visited the Baby Jesus)

Favorite MISSION VIRTUE HERO: St. Francis of Assisi

AMEL invites us to pray in a special way for the MISSION VIRTUE Region of: EUROPE

MISSION VIRTUE HERO:
Francis of Assisi

Francis of Assisi is one of the real-life Mission Virtue Heroes. He lived in the European country of Italy. His life began as a courageous, fun-loving knight. God showed Francis that we discover true wisdom by thinking deeply and seeking the hidden treasures which can be found in poverty and simplicity.

Francis loved reflecting on the humble birth of Baby Jesus so much that he created the first "living nativity scene" with real people and animals. Do you think he included a camel?

*Francis of Assisi
loved celebrating Christmas.*

The wisdom of holy Francis shined in loving service to the God who hid his majesty inside of a baby. Through acts of love, prayer, and sacrifice, wise Francis sought spiritual wealth and delighted in serving the poor. Perhaps you can ask God to grant you the joy and confidence of wisdom, like Francis!

Because of his heroic virtue, many people consider him a saint. Francis of Assissi, please pray for all of us to grow strong in the virtue of WISDOM.

MISSION VIRTUE Prayer Power-UP
Mission Region: EUROPE

We can be Mission Virtue Heroes in two ways. First, we can pray for people who live far away from us. Second, we can pray for people whose souls are far away from Jesus. Let's pray a BIG prayer today for the people with whom Francis of Assisi lived and loved in the land of silver, snowy mountain peaks. Let's pray for everyone living in the Mission Virtue Region of EUROPE. We can pray like this:

> *God, please bless everyone in EUROPE: especially the poor people, the sick people, the sad people, and all of the missionaries who bring Jesus to them. Help all of us to grow in the virtue of WISDOM.*

Meet the creator of Tiny Virtue Heroes™: **Cathy Gilmore**

Author

An award-winning children's author, Cathy is an advocate for virtue. Known as "Mrs. Virtue Lady," Cathy is passionate about assisting parents, grandparents, and teachers to infuse every family with fervent faith and vibrant virtue. Her Tiny Virtue Heroes™ are a menagerie of animal and insect characters who gently model faith and morality. They invite readers of all ages to admire real-life virtue heroes from Christian history.

By energizing the imaginations of children via stories, Cathy is on a quest to place **virtue** at the heart of how kids think of super heroes and super powers. Find out about all the Virtue Heroes™, as well as Cathy's broader efforts to promote virtue, at her website www.VirtueHeroes.com.

Virtue Literacy

Cathy has a passion to promote VIRTUE LITERACY: growth in the knowledge and practice of virtue through the experience of reading and media. Her mission is to empower parents, grandparents, and teachers to help children become virtue-strong through what they read, watch, and listen to. When you buy Tiny Virtue Heroes Books, you are helping in the cause of Virtue Literacy.

Meet the Tiny Virtue Heroes™ Illustrator: **Jeanie Egolf**

Jeanie is the talented artist working to bring Cathy's Virtue Heroes™ characters and storybooks to life. Jeanie has a personal passion to create images that are emotionally engaging for children. Her style integrates a broad spectrum of skills in graphic design, fine art, and children's illustration, enriching her ability to create unique and timeless characters.

The Tiny Virtue Heroes™

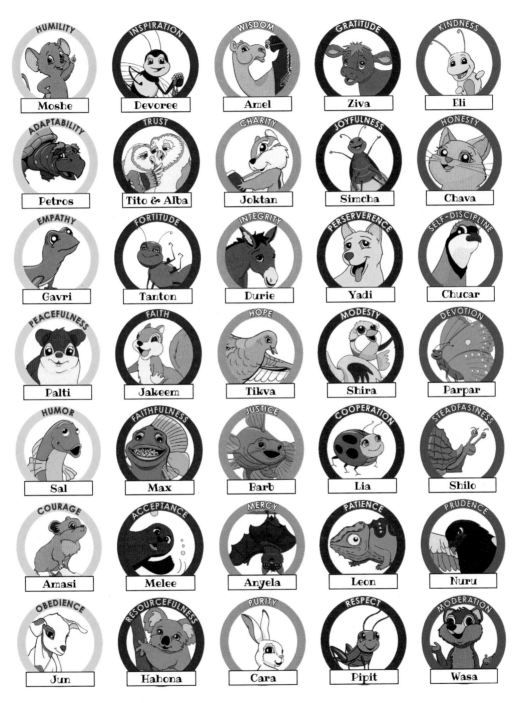

To learn about all these Virtue Heroes™ visit www.VirtueHeroes.com.

Authors depend upon

BOOK REVIEWS!

★ ★ ★ ★ ★

We can't continue our work without
your help. If you've enjoyed this story,
please leave a few words on your favorite
BOOK-REVIEW platform.

Now you're OUR hero!

Made in the USA
Columbia, SC
29 October 2021